Celebrity ?uiz-o-rama™
MUSIC MANIA
Word Seeks, Brain Teasers, and Other Puzzlers!

Celebrity Quiz-o-rama™

Celebrity ?uiz-o-rama™
MUSIC MANIA
Word Seeks, Brain Teasers, and Other Puzzlers!

by Jo Hurley

SCHOLASTIC INC.

New York   Toronto   London   Auckland   Sydney   Mexico City   New Delhi   Hong Kong

This book is unauthorized and is not sponsored by any of the stars included herein, their representatives, or anyone involved with them.

Front Cover: top left: Gail/A.P.R.F./Shooting Star; top right: Joseph Galea; bottom: George Lange/Corbis Outline; **Back Cover:** Khan/Retna; **Insert Page 1:** Ron Davis/Shooting Star; **Insert Page 2:** Joseph Galea (top); A.P.R.F./Deluze/Shooting Star (bottom); **Insert Page 3:** Joseph Galea; **Insert Page 4:** Paul Fenton/Shooting Star (top); Ron Davis/Shooting Star (bottom); **Insert Page 5:** Roba Press/Shooting Star; **Insert Page 6:** Joseph Galea (top); Joseph Galea (bottom); **Insert Page 7:** Joseph Galea; **Insert Page 8:** Bill Reitzel/Corbis Outline.

ISBN 0-439-24409-9

12 11 10 9 8 7 6 5 4 3 2 1   0 1 2 3 4 5 6/0

Printed in the U.S.A.
First Scholastic printing, December 2000
Design: Peter Koblish

TABLE OF CONTENTS

Celebrity ?uiz-o-rama™
MUSIC MANIA
Word Seeks, Brain Teasers, and Other Puzzlers!

INTRODUCTION
Get Puzzled

Just when you think your brain is about to POP . . .

Here are 10 very good reasons you should keep your thoughts on the music makers and shakers and get puzzled . . . *pronto*!

1. Puzzles exercise your little gray cells when you're not hitting the schoolbooks. Unknowingly, you're preparing for the next math test.

2. You can do puzzles with a friend . . . or two. Friendship activities are *always* a bonus!

3. Puzzles practice useless knowledge better than anything! Where else can you be caught discussing the finer points of pop star trivia? Like, nowhere!

4. Seek-and-find puzzles improve your eyesight. OK, maybe not. But that *sounds* good, doesn't it?

5. Crossword puzzles help you learn vocabulary. OK, maybe that's only when the words mean something important. The band member's names from LFO probably don't count.

6. Key knowledge of concert tour locations is as good as any geography lesson. Tell that to your social studies teacher.

7. The uncanny ability to solve code puzzles means that one day you might find yourself in the role of a super-duper spy (or not).

8. If you search and find "cutie-pies" like in

Puzzle 16, you get to take them home! (This is, of course, a *major* lie. How could you possibly think the guys from BBMak would go home with you?)

9. Solving brain teasers makes you hungry — and eating is good!

10. Puzzles are just plain . . . fun! (OK, *that* is your final answer. . . .)

In this mega-book, you'll find everything you need to find, search, circle, cross off, finish, and more. All of the answers are at the back of the book.

The more puzzles you complete . . . the more Pop Points you will be awarded. A Pop Scorecard is also included at the end of the book so you can see how great *you* rate! Pop to it, people! *What are you waiting for?*

PUZZLE 1

The Easiest Puzzle in the Book

Puzzle Value: 2 Pop Points

First of all, are you paying attention? Turn off the TV, put down that Play Station joystick, and stop slurping that soda. This quiz is here to make you focus on the subject at hand . . . and to get you into the puzzle mood, of course.

Identify the items in the top set of boxes on the next page. After you identify each one, follow the line below the picture to the correct box, and write the first letter of its name in that box. Then read the bottom row of boxes across to spell out the subject of this book.

M U S i C

Hey! Throughout the book, you'll find a blank space at the end of each puzzle. This is where you should keep your Pop Points score. Tally it up at the end of the book to get your Pop Totals.

Pop Point Total ___2___

PUZZLE 2

Gone to Pieces

Puzzle Value: 5 Pop Points

Have you been CD shopping lately? Hope so! On the next page are 15 questions. You need to place a three-letter tile into the blank spaces to spell out the correct names of album titles. The matching singers and bands are indicated to help you out! Select tiles from the pile at the bottom of the page. Good luck!

TILE PILE:

~~STR~~	~~WRI~~	~~GAI~~	UPE
WIL	ONE	NIU	CAN
IST	TUR	AGU	IDD
NOW	~~TAC~~	HAD	REA
ERA	PUR	SEL	IUM
TEP	~~OOP~~	VOO	~~ALL~~
RIS	OME	LEN	

? ? ? **Celebrity Quiz-o-rama** ? ? ?

1. NO S T R INGS AT T A C HED ('N Sync)
2. _ _ _DOO (D'Angelo)
3. _ _ _LEN_ _ _ _ M (Will Smith)
4. S_ _ _ _RNA_ _ _ _AL (Santana)
5. M_ _ _LE OF _ _ _HERE (Hanson)
6. 98° and _ _ _ING
7. O P P S . . . I DID IT AG A IN
(Britney Spears)
8. MIL_ _ _ _N _ _ _ _(BSB)
9. S_ _ _ ONE (Steps)
10. S_ _ _ES OF _ _ _PLE (M2M)
11. YOUR_ _ _F OR SOME_ _ _ LIKE
YOU (Matchbox 20)
12. SO _ _ _L (Mandy Moore)
13. _ _ _'T TAKE ME H_ _ _ (Pink)
14. CHR_ _ _INA _ _ _IL_ _ _
(Christina Aguilera)
15. THE W r i TING'S ON THE W a l l
(Destiny's Child)

Pop Point Total _____

PUZZLE 3

Pop Queen Crossword

Puzzle Value: 10 Pop Points

They sing! They dance! They dye their hair weird colors! It's a pop queen *scene* — and most of us are figuring out how to catch up!

How many clues can you solve to fill in the missing parts of the crossword puzzle?

ACROSS

1. Oops! Ever since the *New Mickey Mouse Club,* she's been "Lucky."

3. Norwegian duet with a numeral in their name (and yeah, it's OK to have a numeral in a cross*word*).

7. These chicks are a little bit country. They're the _____ Chicks.

8. Macy _____ was nominated for a Best New Artist Grammy in 2000. (She lost to 10 Across.)

10. She's a genie in a bottle, Christina _____.

12. Tionne Watkins TLC nickname.

13. This diva Mariah sings "Butterfly" and "Fantasy."

14. This "Fair" was started by Sarah McLachlan.

DOWN

1. JC Chasez wrote the song "Bring It All to Me" on their first disc — and their name sounds like a dark color.

2. Lead singer Gwen's hair is in the pink! Name the band.

4. Singing star Alanis has this last name.

5. "Where ____ ____ At?" is a big hit from the group 702.

6. She blows sweet Simpson kisses to Nick Lachey.

9. This Moore's top song rhymes with her first name. Name that tune.

11. They did a 2000 "Can't Help Myself" tour — Nobody's ____ .

Pop Point Total ____

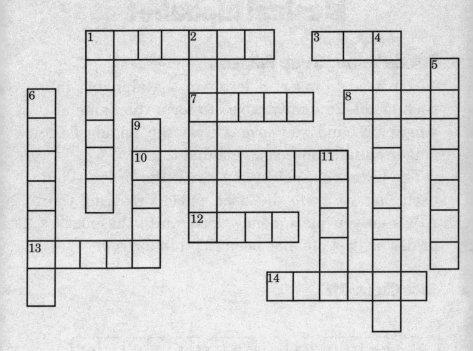

PUZZLE 4

Musical Alphabet

Puzzle Value: 5 Pop Points

You need to insert a letter of the alphabet into each of the 26 empty boxes to form the name of a singer or band you love. Circle the name of the singer or band once you've found it.

The letters are not in any particular order — but each one will only be used once. Cross off your ABCs as you place a new letter into the puzzle's grid. The first one has been filled in for you.

ABCs Check-Off

A	B	C	D	E	F	G	H	I	J	K	L	M
N	O	P	Q	R	S	T	U	V	W	X	**X**	Z

R	B	S	M	A	N	D	Y	M	O	O	R	E	T	S
D	Q	W	I	L	L	S		I	T	H	Q	U	E	E
A	E	T	M	A	R	I		H	C	A	R	E	Y	U
B	M	A	R	S	T	E		S	U	S	O	R	T	B
G	L	I	M	P	B	I		I	T	A	M	I	N	C
U	M	A	R	K	M	C		R	A	T	H	Z	L	E
O	G	L	E	A	N	N		I	M	E	S	S	C	T
G	W	E	N	S	T	E		A	N	I	B	U	B	L
B	R	Q	U	S	I	S		O	L	D	I	S	H	A
E	N	R	I	Q	U	E		G	L	E	S	I	A	S
O	R	N	A	B	R	A		D	Y	S	P	A	R	Z
B	R	I	A	N	L	I		T	R	E	L	L	A	N
D	A	D	R	I	C	H		R	O	N	I	N	A	X
R	S	O	J	B	O	Y		O	N	E	I	A	G	I
H	G	U	A	L	J	E		E	S	T	L	I	F	E
M	I	R	T	L	L	A		R	Y	N	H	I	L	L
G	R	A	E	N	M	A		O	N	N	A	L	I	C
G	O	G	O	O	G	O		D	O	L	L	S	P	A
L	U	R	A	R	I	M		Y	Z	A	B	C	D	Z
C	O	L	O	P	I	N		R	A	Z	Y	F	O	R
B	R	I	T	N	E	Y		P	E	A	R	S	K	A
G	O	O	N	I	C	K		A	C	H	E	Y	G	O
D	R	T	Y	R	E	S		M	G	O	R	G	O	O
N	S	X	N	C	A	B		E	W	E	L	S	E	Z
G	O	O	G	T	R	L		A	N	S	O	N	M	M
G	R	A	I	L	Y	B		M	A	K	A	R	O	N

Pop Point Total _____

POP TEASER A
Night-lights

You are the luckiest duck on the planet. You're sitting in a pop diva's ultra-deluxe hotel room blabbing until all hours. Soon it gets dark outside. There's a terrible storm and just one teeny problem — the hotel's electricity goes out. It flickers on for a second but then . . . oops! It does it again!

Fortunately the hotel has provided for such an emergency: You and the star find an oil lamp, a fireplace, and a large candle.

Unfortunately, you only find one match.

What do you light first?

Give yourself a Pop Point for this one!

Pop Point Total _____

PUZZLE 5

Real Name Code Game

Puzzle Value: 10 Pop Points

Are you a cool code-breaker? These famous singer pseudonyms are so confusing! See how many real names you can reveal by cracking the kooky code. CODE: Each letter is represented by another, *different* letter in the code.

A	B	C	D	E	F	G	H	I	J	K	L	M
L	M	N	O	P	Q	R	S	T	U	V	W	X

N	O	P	Q	R	S	T	U	V	W	X	Y	Z
Y	Z	A	B	C	D	E	F	G	H	I	J	K

1. Alecia Moore is really **ATYV.**
2. Jewel Kilcher is really **UPHPW.**
3. Terius Gray is really **UFGPYTWP.**
4. Jonathan Davis Kamal IV is really **B-ETA.**
5. Shawntae Harris is really **OL MCLE.**

13

6. Eve Jeffers is really **PGP.**

7. Usher Raymond IV is really **FDSPC.**

8. James Todd Smith is really **WW NZZW U.**

9. Marco Antonio Muniz is really **XLCN LYESZYJ.**

10. Mark Andrews is really **DTDBZ.**

11. Aaliyah Haughton is really **LLWTJLS.**

12. Dana Ellane Owens is really **BFPPY WLETQLS.**

13. Love Michelle Harrison is really **NZFCEYPJ WZGP.**

14. Reginald Kenneth Dwight is really **PWEZY UZSY.**

15. Sean Combs is really **AFQQ OLOOJ.**

Pop Point Total _____

PUZZLE 6

Pop-in-the-Blank #1

Puzzle Value: 2 Pop Points

Check this out! A pop star fill-in-the-blank game! You can do this with friends, of course, but you can also do it alone. Just don't look at the story on the next page *yet*! Instead, write the words you need on this chart. Then turn the page, copy them into the story, and see how silly it gets.

Exclamation _____

Noun _____

Boy singing star's name _____

Adjective _____

Name of teacher _____

Place _____

Part of the body _____

Same singing star's name _____

Funny noun _____

Something you collect _____

? ? ? Celebrity Quiz-o-rama™ ? ? ?

TV show _____

Number _____

Major event _____

Same singing star's name_____

Girl singing star's name_____

One more girl star's name _____

Adjective _____

I LOVE A POP STAR

_____! I *really* wanted to go to a
exclamation

_____ to see _____, my
noun   boy singing star's name

favorite pop star. But Mom said, "No way." My

_____ mom wanted me to go with
adjective

_____ to the _____
name of teacher   place

instead. What!? I couldn't believe

my_____. Didn't she understand how
part of the body

16

PUZZLE 6

I felt about_____ ? I listened to every
  same singing star's name

_____ that star made! I collected
  funny noun

_____ of that star, I watched his
  something you collect

episodes of _____ , and I even
  TV show

traveled _____ miles once to see that
  number

star appearing at a _____.
  major event

_____ was way better than
  same singing star's name

_____ and _____.
  girl singing star's name   one more girl star's name

Sometimes Moms just don't get it! Pop stars make
the world a _____ place!
  adjective

Pop Point Total _____

PUZZLE 7

Pop Singer Remix

Puzzle Value: 10 Pop Points

You probably have never heard of these crazy singers. That's because their names are all mixed up! Change one letter in each word to form the *correct* name of a popular singer.

1. TAILOR HANGON _____

2. DEVIL LIME _____ (from LFO)

3. RUFF BADDY _____

4. BARON CARVER _____

5. CANDY MOORS _____ ·

6. ROCKY MARLIN _____

7. DANCE LASS _____ (from 'N Sync)

8. FELINE LION _____

9. NICE DARTER _____ (from Backstreet Boys)

10. PARIAH CARED _____

Pop Point Total _____

POP TEASER B
Beat the Band

You and a friend have decided to attend a super-duper band contest. Competing for the title of "Best Band in the Land" are some of your faves: 98°, BBMAK, BACKSTREET BOYS, 'N SYNC, and NO AUTHORITY.

98° finishes in front of BBMAK, but behind the Backstreet Boys. 'N SYNC finishes in front of NO AUTHORITY but behind BBMAK.

What was the final ranking of the contest winners?

Give yourself 3 Pop Points if you answered correctly.

1st place _BSB_
2nd place _98°_
3rd place _BBMac_
4th place _N'sync_
5th place _No Authority_

Pop Point Total _3_

PUZZLE 8

Video Scramble

Puzzle Value: 10 Pop Points

How well do you know your music videos? Unscramble the names of the bands and singers that belong to the clues below.

1. This material girl dances around in front of an American flag singing a tune about a very American dessert.
ODNAMNA _____

2. The lead singer and his band mates crash into an office building to find out "How It's Gonna Be."
DIRTH YEE DILNB _____

3. In her video, a mother and daughter "turn" to each other after a car crash in the rain.
TRIHCNASI AAIEULRG _____

4. She sings a song to honor high school graduates — and all your friends forever.
TACNIMIV _____

PUZZLE 8

5. They're dressed up like puppets even though they claim to have no strings attached when they sing "Bye, Bye, Bye."
SCNNY _____

6. First she wears a red catsuit and *then* she gets a gift from a cute astronaut.
TYNRIEB EPSSAR _____

7. This trio is singing for their supper "Back Here" in a London metro station.
KMBAB _____

8. This Latin singer shakes it up onstage with a band and some dancing ladies as they shake their bon bons. YRKIC MIANTR _____

9. These fine singers move from room to room posing while they "Say My Name."
SSNIEDYT IDCLH _____

10. Why is this *non*-dumb blonde rolling around in the snow in this video from the movie *Snow Day*?
UHOK _____

11. These three brothers filmed "This Time Around" in New Orleans in the middle of the night
SOAHNN _____

Pop Point Total _____

PUZZLE 9

Bands on the Run

Puzzle Value: 15 Pop Points

Your favorite pop stars are hitting the concert scene! Can you place the correct words into the puzzle... and send your best bands on the road with style?

3 letters
ACT
PAY
POP

4 letters
OPEN
OVER
SEAT
TECH

5 letters
ENTER
LEVEL
MUSIC
STAGE

6 letters
TICKET

7 letters
ANAHEIM
ATLANTA
CENTERS
ORLANDO
SOLD OUT
STADIUM
THEATER

8 letters
COLISEUM
NO REFUND

9 letters
SUPERDOME

10 letters
AUDITORIUM

11 letters
NEW YORK CITY
PERFORMANCE

PUZZLE 9

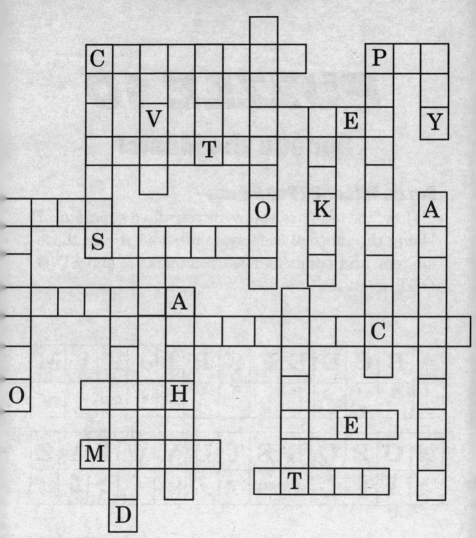

Pop Point Total _____

PUZZLE 10

Decode the Music!

Puzzle Value: 20 Pop Points

How "in tune" are you with your fave superstars?
Using the musical code system below, reveal these
singers' and bands' one-word names . . . and SING
OUT about it!

A	B	C	D	E	F	G	H	I	J	K	L	M

N	O	P	Q	R	S	T	U	V	W	X	Y	Z

Check out the answers in the answer key.

This 'N Sync-er has his own charitable organization: What's it called?

Guess how this singer/songwriter got her nickname?

Brandy goes only by her first name — do you know her last name?

He's Aaron Carter.
What group is his older brother in?

Britney Spears has her own:
a) doll b) gum c) clothing line

In TLC's hit song, "No Scrubs,"
what's a scrub?

'N Sync: Of these singles, which hit #1?
a) "Tearin' Up My Heart"   b) "Bye Bye Bye"
c) "God Must Have Spent a Little More Time on You"

Jessica Simpson dueted on a song with Nick Lachey from what teen movie weeper?

Which two guys in 98° are brothers?

Could Westlife be any cuter? What European country do these lads hail from?

What major award did Christina Aguilera
win in 2000?

1. ♪ 𝅝 ♪ ♪ 𝄽 PINK

2. *mp* 𝄐 𝅝 𝅗𝅥 ♪ ♪ 1STING

3. ♩ ♩ ¢ 𝅝 ♪ ♩ ♪ AALIYAY

4. ♪ ♭ ♪ *sf* ♭ ♪ ♩

5. 𝄐 ¢ ♩

6. ♩ 𝅝 ⌣ 𝄐 ♩

7. ¢ ♩ ♭

8. 𝅝 ♪ ♪ ♪ ♭ *mp* ♩ ♪ ♪ *mp* ♩

9. ♪ ♩ ♪ *mp* ♭ ♪

10. *f* *mp* ♪ ♪ ♩ ♯

25

POP TEASER C
Robber

Susie lives with her family in New York City. Last week, while her family was out, Susie's next-door neighbor came over to spend the evening. At one point, the neighbor stepped out for just a moment to get something at the store.

After the neighbor left, Susie heard a knock at the door. Suddenly, the members of a popular band came inside and started to raid the refrigerator.

Susie had never seen the singers before, and they had no right to be in her living room, but she did nothing to stop them. In fact, she didn't even act surprised by their actions.

Why not?

Give yourself a Pop Point if you can figure this one out.

Pop Point Total _____

PUZZLE 11

You Wanna?

Puzzle Value: 5 Pop Points

Do *"you wanna"* fill in the missing words in these same-sounding song titles? In the hit song titles below, the words *"you"* and *"wanna"* are used a lot! Use the numbered code to solve this one! The singer and band names are here to help you out, too.

CODE: Each letter is represented by a number.

A	B	C	D	E	F	G	H	I	J	K	L	M
1	2	3	4	5	6	7	8	9	10	11	12	13

N	O	P	Q	R	S	T	U	V	W	X	Y	Z
14	15	16	17	18	19	20	21	22	23	24	25	26

? ? ? Celebrity Quiz-o-rama™ ? ? ?

1. 9 4/15/14/20 **WANNA** 11/9/19/19 **YOU**
7/15/15/4/14/9/7/8/20 (sung by LFO)

2. 20/8/5/18/5 **YOU** 7/15 (sung by Pink)

3. 9 **WANNA** 12/15/22/5 **YOU**
6/15/18/5/22/5/18 (sung by Jessica Simpson)

4. 23/8/1/20 9 **WANNA** 4/15
(sung by No Authority)

5. 9/12/12 2/5 7/15/15/4 20/15 **YOU**
(sung by 'N Sync)

6. 20/8/1/20/19 23/8/1/20 **YOU** 7/5/20
(sung by Boyz and Girlz United)

7. 9/6 **YOU** **WANNA** 4/1/14/3/5
(sung by Nobody's Angel)

8. 20/8/1/14/11 7/15/4 9 6/15/21/14/4 **YOU**
(sung by Mariah Carey with Joe and 98°)

9. 9 20/21/18/14 20/15 **YOU**
(sung by Christina Aguilera)

PUZZLE 11

10. 13/9/19/19 **YOU**   12/9/11/5   3/18/1/26/25
(sung by The Moffatts)

11. 9/6 **YOU**   8/1/4   13/25   12/15/22/5
(sung by Jennifer Lopez)

12. 9 **WANNA**   2/5   23/9/20/8 **YOU**
(sung by Mandy Moore)

Pop Point Total _____

PUZZLE 12

Cross Outs

Puzzle Value: 10 Pop Points (5 points for each grid you get right!)

Follow the cross-out instructions for each teeny grid. When you've crossed off the right stuff, you'll reveal letters that spell a super pop singer's or band's name! Good luck!

1. Cross off all vowels except A and Y.
2. Cross off all letters that come between F and L.
3. Cross off all letters in the first column.
4. What letters are left? ___ ___ ___ ___ ___ ___

Q	E	U	I	O
R	B	G	H	J
S	K	R	A	E
T	J	N	D	U
B	U	K	H	Y

PUZZLE 12

1. Cross off all 4 corners.
2. Cross off all E's, I's, and O's.
3. Cross off all the X's marking the spot.
4. What letters are left?

___ ___ ___ ___ ___   ___ ___ ___

S	S	E	U	U
I	G	X	E	A
O	X	X	X	I
R	X	O	X	R
A	A	E	Y	Y

Pop Point Total _____

31

PUZZLE 13

Musical Disguises

Puzzle Value: 10 Pop Points

Heads up! These names of instruments and other musical words are hidden in the sentences below:

Concert
Song
Harmony
Notes
Radio
Chorus
Strings
Horn
Bass
Lyric

Can you find and underline them? The first one has been done for you.

1. The members of Westlife showed a lot of c**harm on y**esterday's tour stop.

2. In today's mail I saw a concert tour ad. I opened the envelope, and I found free tickets inside.

3. Wherever Hanson goes to play, I will follow!

4. Out of all the guys in LFO, only Rich Cronin makes me swoon!

5. Sometimes music-mixers have to dub, assuming they're adding in sound effects.

6. Whom do I like best in 'N Sync? JC on certain days and Justin on other days.

7. I have no tests this week, so I am going to watch *lots* of MTV.

8. I can't decide whether I want to buy that new disc from Aaliyah or not.

9. Christina Aguilera wears the best rings, bracelets, and other jewelry!

10. Do the boys in 98° like to sing more for kids at the beach or us?

And how about the singers who have the musical words in their names *already*? Give it up for Lance **Bass,** Joey Fa**tone,** and Kid **Rock!**

Pop Point Total _____

POP TEASER D
Thirsty

A popular girl singer, Girl A, walks into a health food restaurant and asks for a glass of water. Another famous female pop star, Girl B, ducks behind the counter. Moments later, she leaps out, taking Girl A by surprise.

"Aaaaah!" Girl A jumps with shock.

Then Girl A thanks Girl B and walks out.

Is Girl B crazy? Is Girl A scared off by the pop competition?

What's UP?

Give yourself a Pop Point if you know the deal.

Pop Point Total _____

PUZZLE 14

Pop Star Memory Test

Puzzle Value: 10 Pop Points

How good is *your* memory? Before you read any further, take a quick look back at the color pages in this book. Pay attention to what the stars are wearing, how they're sitting, and who they're with! When you've taken a good look, come back to this page and take the test.

1. In the cool pic of Justin Timberlake, is he wearing something around his neck?

a. Yup.

b. Nope.

c. I can't see his neck.

2. Is pretty Pink wearing something on her head?

a. Nothin' there but pink hair.

b. You bet—she's sporting a scarf.

c. That's a hat!

? ? ? Celebrity Quiz-o-rama™ ? ? ?

3. What pattern is cutie Aaron Carter wearing on his shirt?

 a. Stripes
 b. Polka dots
 c. Checks

4. In her photo, how did Britney have the hair stylist do her 'do?

 a. Long and straight
 b. Up, up, up!
 c. Braids, please

5. Check out the guys from 'N Sync! In what order (left to right) are they standing?

 a. Lance, Justin, Chris, JC, and Joey
 b. Joey, Justin, JC, Chris, and Lance
 c. JC, Lance, Joey, Justin, and Chris

6. Which one of the 'N Sync hotties is wearing a white T-shirt?

 a. Justin
 b. Joey
 c. JC

PUZZLE 14

7. Look at TLC! Which of these Grammy-winning divas has a tattoo you can see in the photograph?
a. Left Eye
b. T-Boz
c. Chili

8. Is Brandy wearing sunglasses?
a. No way! She's all eyes.
b. Yes! She's made in the shade.
c. No, but she's wearing goggles.

9. What is the *so real* color of Christina's shirt?
a. Black
b. Yellow
c. Red

10. In the photo of Westlife, how can you ID lead singer Shane?
a. He's wearing a red sweater.
b. He's wearing a dress.
c. He's wearing a hockey mask.

? ? ? Celebrity Quiz-o-rama™ ? ? ?

11. What's special about Jessica Simpson's outfit?
a. Her shirt has long sleeves.
b. Her shirt has ruffled sleeves.
c. Her shirt has no sleeves.

12. The boys from 98° are here to say hello to you! Where are they standing in the photo?
a. On the beach.
b. Coming off a bus.
c. On top of Old Smokey.

Pop Point Total _____

PUZZLE 15

Who Wants to Be a Music Maniac?

Puzzle Value: 20 Pop Points (because these are tough!)

This is a pop quiz for the kings and queens of total trivial knowledge. In the category of "utterly useless," here are the questions. Drumroll, please!

1. This band's lead singer, Jonathan Davis, used to be an assistant coroner (which means he worked with *dead* bodies — ugh!).
  a. Third Eye Blind
  b. No Doubt
  c. Backstreet Boys

2. This 98° singer takes his camera with him everywhere because black-and-white photography is a major hobby.
  a. Drew Lachey
  b. Brad Fischetti
  c. Nick Carter

39

? ? ? Celebrity Quiz-o-rama™ ? ? ?

3. Who cut his hair before the release of his band's second album, *This Time Around*?
a.   Shane Filan
b.   Taylor Hanson
c.   Justin Timberlake

4. This band started out in Orlando, Florida.
a.   'N Sync
b.   Backstreet Boys
c.   A and B

5.   This band (who had a hit with "Walkin' on the Sun") sounds like someone hit 'em in the face.
a.   Third Eye Blind
b.   98°
c.   Smash Mouth

6. She wrote a book with her mom, Lynne, called *Heart to Heart*.
a.   Mandy Moore
b.   Britney Spears
c.   Christina Aguilera

7. This 'N Sync cutie says he has more than 70 pairs of sneakers in his collection!
   a. Justin Timberlake
   b. Lance Bass
   c. Chris Kirkpatrick

8. Even though he had major heart surgery as a kid, this BSB babe is still a major basketball player and fan.
   a. Brian Littrell
   b. Kian Egan
   c. Justin Timberlake

9. It's all in the family with this girl band. Britney Spears was once a member before she flew solo and 'N Sync's Justin Timberlake's mom, Lynn, is their manager!
   a. Destiny's Child
   b. TLC
   c. Innosense

Pop Point Total _____

PUZZLE 16

Cutie-pie Word Search

Puzzle Value: 50 Pop Points

Some of the cutest hunks in pop music are hidden in the word search on page 44. Find the names shown in bold capital letters in the lists below and on the next page. Look up, down, backward, diagonally. First and last names are hidden in different places in the puzzle and short names like Abs and A. J. may appear more than once. When every name has been located, what single letter remains in all the uncircled squares?

'N Sync
JUSTIN Timberlake
LANCE BASS
Joey **FATONE**
J. C. **CHASEZ**
CHRIS KIRKPATRICK

LFO
BRAD Fischetti
RICH CRONIN
DEVIN LIMA

IMx
JEROME Jones
Marques **HOUSTON**
KELTON Kessee

Westlife
MARK Feehily
KIAN Egan
SHANE FILAN
BRYAN McFadden
NICKY BYRNE

PUZZLE 16

98°
Nick **LACHEY**
Jeff **TIMMONS**
DREW Lachey
Justin **JEFFRE**

Backstreet Boys
A. J. **MCLEAN**
Nick **CARTER**
Brian **LITTRELL**
HOWIE Dorough
KEVIN Richardson

Five
Rich **NEVILLE**
SCOTT Robinson
ABS BREEN
SEAN CONLON
J BROWN

BBMak
Mark **BARRY**
STEVEN McNally
CHRISTIAN BURNS

C-Note
DAVID Perez
Brody **MARTINEZ**
RAUL Molina
DRU Rogers

No Authority
DANNY ZAVATSKY
Ricky **GODINEZ**
ERIC Stretch
TOMMY McCarthy

Solo Cute Guys
RICKY Martin
MARC Anthony
Enrique **IGLESIAS**
WILL Smith
AARON Carter
Michael **FREDO**

5 Bonus Pop Points:
What letter remains?

———————————

Pop Point Total ———————

E	B	A	R	R	Y	K	S	T	A	V	A	Z	B	B	E
N	E	V	E	T	S	R	I	C	H	S	N	R	U	B	N
R	A	O	B	C	H	A	S	E	Z	B	B	Y	K	A	A
Y	T	Y	D	T	I	M	M	O	N	S	L	K	I	S	H
B	O	N	R	E	N	O	T	A	F	B	L	C	R	S	S
K	M	R	A	B	R	A	D	Z	B	A	E	I	K	C	B
I	M	L	A	E	R	F	F	E	J	A	R	R	P	O	B
A	Y	A	J	U	S	T	I	N	M	U	T	B	A	T	F
N	H	C	R	M	L	B	G	I	R	B	T	E	T	T	I
A	O	H	B	C	L	N	L	D	A	V	I	D	R	N	L
I	U	E	N	L	E	I	E	O	K	W	L	C	I	E	A
T	S	Y	I	E	R	V	S	G	O	E	A	B	C	E	N
S	T	W	N	A	I	E	I	H	B	R	L	B	K	R	E
I	O	B	O	N	C	K	A	B	T	D	B	T	B	B	C
R	N	O	R	A	A	B	S	E	N	O	L	N	O	C	N
H	N	I	C	K	Y	D	R	E	L	L	I	V	E	N	A
C	B	M	A	R	T	I	N	E	Z	B	R	O	W	N	L

PUZZLE 17

Musical Math

Puzzle Value: 5 Pop Points

Maybe you're not great at math class . . . but that doesn't mean you can't make these pop star numbers add up.

1. The members of Boyz 'n' Girlz United had lunch with the Backstreet Boys. How many people ate together?

a. 7
b. 8
c. 9

2. Add 5 to the number of girls in Nobody's Angel and then subtract the number of members in Hanson. What number do you have?

a. 4
b. 6
c. 8

PUZZLE 17

3. 98° *plus* A*Teen *plus* TLC equals how many people?

   a. 9
   b. 10
   c. 11

4. Add the number of members in BBMak to the members in LFO and then multiply it by the members of M2M. How many do you get?

   a. 8
   b. 10
   c. 12

5. Sisqo´, Mariah Carey, Hanson, Britney Spears, No Doubt, and 'N Sync were all hanging out. How many chairs were needed for everyone to have a seat?

   a. 14
   b. 6
   c. 15

Pop Point Total _____

PUZZLE 18

Pop-in-the-Blank #2

Puzzle Value: 2 Pop Points

It's another superstar fill-in-the-blank game. Remember: Don't look at the story on the next page yet! Instead, write the words you need on this chart. Then turn the page, copy them into the story, and have fun!

Pop star name_____

Time of day_____

Action word ending in -ing _____

Something in nature _____

Friend's name_____

Action word_____

Room in your house _____

Your town_____

Large number_____

Article of clothing _____

Article of clothing _____

Unit of time _____

Adjective _____

Action word _____

Animal _____

POP FAN LETTER

Dear _____,
pop star name

I wake up every day at _____ and listen to
time of day

your CD. My favorite song that you sing is

" _____ "

_____ on Top of the _____.
action word ending in -ing   something in nature

Wow, it really rocks! My best friend _____
friend's name

"
likes _____ in the _____ better, but
action word   room in your house "

whatever. When are you coming to sing in

_____? I would pay _____
your town   large number

dollars to see you in concert — I swear! I have a

PUZZLE 18

poster of you wearing _____ and
article of clothing

_____ on my bedroom wall, and I look at it
article of clothing

every _____. I think you are just
unit of time

soooooo _____! You make me _____!
adjective   action word

I feel like a(n) _____ when I listen to your
animal

music. Thank you sooooo much!

Pop Point Total _____

PUZZLE 19

The Pop Stars Are Missing!

Puzzle Value: 5 Pop Points for each correct answer — WOW!

Some letters have been omitted from the alphabets below. Unscramble the missing letters to form the names of singing stars in all 10 questions. Good luck!

1. ABCDFGIJKLMNOPQTVWXYZ_____
2. ABCDEFGHJLMOQRSTUVWXYZ_____
3. BCEFGHIJKLOPQRSTUVWXZ_____
4. ACDFGHJKLMOPQSUVWXZ_____
5. ABCDFHIJKLMOPQRSTUVXYZ_____
6. ABCDEFGIJLMNPQRSTVWXYZ_____
7. ABCDEFGHKLMOPQRVWXYZ_____
8. CEFGHIJKLMOPQSTUVWXZ_____
9. BDFGHIJKMOPQRSTUVWXYZ_____
10. ABCDFGJKLMNPQRSTUVXYZ_____

Pop Point Total _____

POP TEASER E
On the Road

Two superstars were on the road when they ran into each other. They were staying at the same hotel and had rooms right next to each other!

Both guy singers were totally exhausted, but Singer A just couldn't get to sleep. Eventually around two o'clock in the morning, he called down to the hotel operator and asked to be put through to the next room where Singer B was sleeping.

As soon as the phone rang, Singer B woke up. He picked up the phone immediately, but Singer A hung up without saying a word. After that, Singer A was able to fall right to sleep.

Explain what happened.

Give yourself a Pop Point if you know the deal.

Pop Point Total _____

PUZZLE 20

Pop-o-matic

Puzzle Value: 20 Pop Points automatically! Isn't that *nice*? Yeah, well, the end of the book is coming, so . . .

Which pop star are you most like? Set the record straight by answering the questions below. Check out the Answer Key to check your pop star status.

1. Your closet probably contains:

a.   black boots and glitter nail polish.

b.   neon tube tops and Skechers.

c.   clean, white T-shirts.

2. You'd rather spend your time over the weekend:

a.   playing Sega, blasting the stereo, and having a party!

b.   hanging at the mall.

c.   with your parents or playing sports.

PUZZLE 20

3. If you rented a video to watch with your BFF, you'd see:

a. anything starring Adam Sandler.

b. *Ten Things I Hate About You*

c. *The Little Mermaid.*

4. On your CD player, you are always listening to:

a. No Doubt, no doubt!

b. Christina Aguilera or Britney's dance tunes

c. Jessica and Nick's "Where You Are"

5. On TV, you are always watching:

a. *Malcolm in the Middle*

b. *Dawson's Creek*

c. *Moesha*

Pop Point Total _____

PUZZLE 21

Pop Grid

Puzzle Value: 25 Pop Points because you've been such a great puzzler! Thanks for playing, pop fan!

You're always humming your favorite pop tunes, right? Now is your chance to find all the right words to the songs you love so much. Hidden in the puzzle grid on page 56 are the words from some of the coolest tunes around. They can be up, down, horizontal, or backward — but not diagonal. Find 'em all or else the puzzle won't work. You're looking for the words in bold capital letters.

When you're done, there will be a few letters remaining. Those letters, in order, will spell a secret question just for you. Answer it — or else!

Let's get quizzical *one more time!*

MISS You **LIKE CRAZY** (The Moffatts)

C'est La **VIE** (B*witched)

SLAM Dunk (Da Funk) (Five)

RAY of **LIGHT** (Madonna)

WALK Me **HOME** (Mandy Moore)

The **HARDEST** Thing (98°)

SHOW Me the **MEANING** of Being **LONELY** (BSB)

This **TIME** Around (Hanson)

TRY Again (Aaliyah)

STAY the **NIGHT** (IMx)

That's What You **GET** (Boyz 'n' Girlz United)

BRING It All To Me (Blaque)

Get in **LINE** (Barenaked Ladies)

SWEAR It Again (Westlife)

BACK Here (BBMak)

LUCKY (Britney Spears)

It's **ALRIGHT** (Five)

? ? ? Celebrity Quiz-o-rama™ ? ? ?

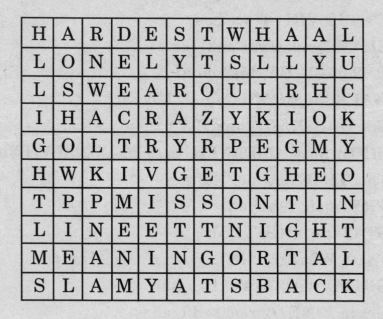

H	A	R	D	E	S	T	W	H	A	A	L
L	O	N	E	L	Y	T	S	L	L	Y	U
L	S	W	E	A	R	O	U	I	R	H	C
I	H	A	C	R	A	Z	Y	K	I	O	K
G	O	L	T	R	Y	R	P	E	G	M	Y
H	W	K	I	V	G	E	T	G	H	E	O
T	P	P	M	I	S	S	O	N	T	I	N
L	I	N	E	E	T	T	N	I	G	H	T
M	E	A	N	I	N	G	O	R	T	A	L
S	L	A	M	Y	A	T	S	B	A	C	K

And the mystery question is . . .

__ __ __ __ ' __   __ __ __ __   __ __ __

__ __ __ __ __   __ __ __ __ __ ?

Pop Point Total _____

ANSWER KEY

Back Cover Answers: Aaliyah's real name is Aaliyah Haughton; The band is 'N Sync; 98° plus A*Teen plus TLC= 10 people.

Photo Quiz Answers: Justin's charitable organization is The Justin Timberlake Foundation; Pink got her name because of her pink hair; Brandy's last name is Norwood; Aaron Carter's older brother Nick Carter is in Backstreet Boys; Britney Spears has her own (a) doll and (b) gum; in TLC's hit song, "No Scrubs," a scrub is a slacker; of the three 'N Sync singles listed, just (b) "Bye Bye Bye" hit #1; Jessica Simpson sang the duet with Nick Lachey from 98°; in 98°, Nick and Drew Lachey (the top two guys in the pic) are brothers; Westlife could not possibly be any cuter — they are already as cute as can be! And they are from Ireland; Christina Aguilera won the Grammy for best new artist in 2000.

Puzzle 1: The Easiest Puzzle in the World
The word is MUSIC.

? ? ? **Celebrity Quiz-o-rama**™ ? ? ?

Puzzle 2: Gone to Pieces

1. NO STRINGS ATTACHED
2. VOODOO
3. WILLENNIUM
4. SUPERNATURAL
5. PLAY
6. 98° AND RISING
7. OOPS . . . I DID IT AGAIN
8. MILLENNIUM
9. STEP ONE
10. SHADES OF PURPLE
11. YOURSELF OR SOMEONE LIKE YOU
12. SO REAL
13. CAN'T TAKE ME HOME
14. CHRISTINA AGUILERA
15. THE WRITING'S ON THE WALL

Puzzle 3: Pop Queen Crossword

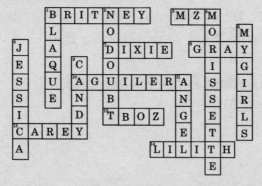

ANSWER KEY

Puzzle 4: Musical Alphabet

Pop Teaser A: Night-lights

You light the match, *silly!*

Puzzle 5: Real Name Code Game

1. Pink
2. Jewel
3. Juvenile
4. Q-Tip

? ? ? Celebrity Quiz-o-rama™ ? ? ?

5. Da Brat
6. Eve
7. Usher
8. LL Cool J
9. Marc Anthony
10. Sisqó
11. Aaliyah
12. Queen Latifah
13. Courtney Love
14. Elton John
15. Puff Daddy

Puzzle 6: Pop-in-the-Blank #1
There are no right answers! Anything you put in the blanks is A-OK!

Puzzle 7: Pop Singer ReMix
1. TAYLOR HANSON
2. DEVIN LIMA
3. PUFF DADDY
4. AARON CARTER
5. MANDY MOORE
6. RICKY MARTIN
7. LANCE BASS
8. CELINE DION

ANSWER KEY

9. NICK CARTER
10. MARIAH CAREY

Pop Teaser B: Beat the Band
1st place: BACKSTREET BOYS
2nd place: 98°
3rd place: BBMAK
4th place: 'N SYNC
5th place: NO AUTHORITY

Puzzle 8: Video Scramble
1. MADONNA
2. THIRD EYE BLIND
3. CHRISTINA AGUILERA
4. VITAMIN C
5. 'N SYNC
6. BRITNEY SPEARS
7. BBMAK
8. RICKY MARTIN
9. DESTINY'S CHILD
10. HOKU
11. HANSON

Puzzle 9: Bands on the Run

```
                      S
        C O L I S E U M       P O P
        E       E   P         E   A Y
        N   E   E   E   N T E R   Y
        T H E A T E R   I     F
        E       L   R   C     O
    O V E R         D   K     R         A
    R       S T A D I U M     M         U
    L       C       E   T     A         D
    A T L A N T A       S     N         I
    N       O   N E W Y O R K C I T Y
    D       R   A       L     E   O
    O     T E C H       D     O   R
          F   H         O P E N   I
        M U S I C       U         U
          N   M     S T A G E     M
          D
```

Puzzle 10: Decode the Music!

1. PINK
2. STING
3. AALIYAH
4. BOYZONE
5. TLC
6. FIVE
7. LFO
8. INNOSENSE
9. HANSON
10. USHER

Pop Teaser C: Robber

Susie is a goldfish.

ANSWER KEY

Puzzle 11: You Wanna?

1. I DON'T **WANNA** KISS **YOU** GOODNIGHT
2. THERE **YOU** GO
3. I **WANNA** LOVE **YOU** FOREVER
4. WHAT I **WANNA** DO
5. I'LL BE GOOD TO **YOU**
6. THAT'S WHAT **YOU** GET
7. IF **YOU WANNA** DANCE
8. THANK GOD I FOUND **YOU**
9. I TURN TO **YOU**
10. MISS **YOU** LIKE CRAZY
11. IF **YOU** HAD MY LOVE
12. I **WANNA** BE WITH **YOU**

Puzzle 12: Cross Outs

First Grid: Second Grid:

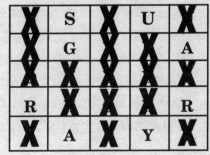

BRANDY   SUGAR RAY

? ? ? Celebrity Quiz-o-rama™ ? ? ?

Puzzle 13: Musical Disguises

1. The members of Westlife showed a lot of c**harm on y**esterday's tour stop. (harmony)

2. In today's mail I saw a concert tou**r ad. I o**pened the envelope, and I found free tickets inside. (radio)

3. Wherever Han**son g**oes to play, I will follow! (song)

4. Out of all the guys in LFO, on**ly Ric**h Cronin makes me swoon! (lyric)

5. Sometimes music-mixers have to du**b, ass**uming they're adding in sound effects. (bass)

6. Whom do I like best in 'N Sync? J**C on cer-t**ain days and Justin on other days. (concert)

7. I have **no tes**ts this week, so I am going to watch *lots* of MTV. (notes)

8. I can't decide whether I want to buy that new disc from Aaliya**h or n**ot. (horn)

9. Christina Aguilera wears the be**st rings,** bracelets, and other jewelry! (strings)

10. Do the boys in 98° like to sing more for kids at the bea**ch or us**? (chorus)

Pop Teaser D: Thirsty

Girl A had the hiccups. She thought she needed a

glass of water to cure them, but getting scared by Girl B did the trick instead.

Puzzle 14: Pop Star Memory Test

1. (a) Yup.
2. (c) That's a hat!
3. (c) Checks
4. (a) Long and straight
5. (c) JC, Lance, Joey, Justin, and Chris
6. (a) Justin
7. (a) Left Eye
8. (a) No way! She's all eyes.
9. (a) Black
10. (a) He's wearing a red sweater.
11. (c) Her shirt has no sleeves.
12. (b) Coming off a bus.

Puzzle 15: Who Wants to Be a Music Maniac?

1. (a) Third Eye Blind
2. (a) Drew Lachey
3. (b) Taylor Hanson
4. (c) A and B
5. (c) Smash Mouth
6. (b) Britney Spears
7. (b) Lance Bass

? ? ? Celebrity Quiz-o-rama™ ? ? ?

8. (a) Brian Littrell

9. (c) Innosense

Puzzle 16: Cutie-pie Word Search

What letter remains? B (for cutie-pie . . . BOYS!)

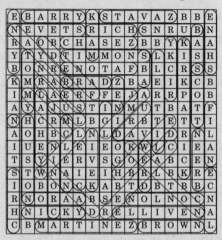

Puzzle 17: Musical Math

1. (c) There are 4 members of Boyz 'n' Girlz United and 5 members of BSB. 4+5=9

2. (b) There are 4 girls in Nobody's Angel and 3 members in Hanson. 5+4=9. 9-3=6.

3. (b) There are 4 guys in 98°, 3 members of A*Teen, and 3 members of TLC. 4+3+3=10.

4. (c) There are 3 members in both BBMak and LFO, and 2 members in LFO. 3+3=6. 6x2=12.

5. (a) Sisqó, Mariah, and Britney are all solo. There are 3 members in both No Doubt and Hanson and 5 members in 'N Sync. 1+1+1+3+3+5=14.

Puzzle 18: Pop-in-the-Blank #2
There are no right answers! Anything you put in the blanks is A-OK!

Puzzle 19: The Pop Stars Are Missing!
1. USHER
2. PINK
3. MANDY
4. BRITNEY
5. GWEN
6. HOKU
7. JUSTIN
8. BRANDY
9. LANCE
10. HOWIE

Pop Teaser D: On the Road
Singer B was snoring and it was keeping singer A awake. He called down to the hotel operator so the call could wake up the snoring B, and give singer A a little peace and quiet. Zzzzzzzz . . .

Puzzle 20: Pop-o-matic

If you answered mostly **As** — You're a wild child through and through! You've got the super, dare-to-be-different traits of Sisqó, Christina, and TLC.

If you answered mostly **Bs** — You're practical, down to earth, and fun! You've got the spunky side of Britney, BSB, and Pink.

If you answered mostly **Cs** — You're sweetness all over! You've got the cute smile and big heart of Jessica Simpson, M2M, and The Moffatts.

Puzzle 21: Pop Grid

```
H A R D E S T W H A A L
L O N E L Y T S L L Y U
L S W E A R O U I R H C
I H A C R A Z Y K I O K
G O L T R Y R P E G M Y
H W K I V G E T G H E O
T P P M I S S O N T I N
L I N E E T T N I G H T
M E A N I N G O R T A L
S L A M Y A T S B A C K
```

And the mystery question is . . .

WHAT'S YOUR POP POINT TOTAL? ———

POP POINT
SCORECARD

You made it through all the games and quizzes! Way to go! Now it's time to go back and count up your pop points. Check out the next page to see how you rate.

POP POINT TOTAL   POP RATING

0–20 SUGAR-FREE POP
You have a teeny bit of pop fizz, but in general you're not all that sweet on the pop-stats! Maybe you should pay a little more attention to the music charts, tune in to the radio stations, and check out the latest *Billboard* chart. Soon enough you just might be able to tell Britney, Jessica, and Mandy apart!

21–60   POP WANNABE
You're good with those word searches and pop-in-the-blanks, aren't you? You've gotten your points together with the basics, but it's time to get all the facts together! Pop perfection comes to those who

? ? ? Celebrity Quiz-o-rama™ ? ? ?

pay attention to fads, trends, and all the tunes on MTV!

61–100   POP KNOW-IT-ALL

Sure, you know some of the pop music star basics, but you have a little way to go! You know a major hottie when you see one — like Justin Timberlake or Christina Aguilera — but as far as the rest of the pop stars go . . . you're not exactly in the know. Give it a little time and soon you might be pop-tacular!

101–146   DON'T STOP POP

You've been practicing your pop trivia, haven't you? Of all your friends, you're the clever one who knows the members of Westlife (even with those Irish names!) and all the lyrics to Britney's, "Oops, I Did It Again," but guess what? You're not at the tip-top . . . *yet*. . . .

147–infinity   TIP-TOP POP

You got so many points that you almost *popped* off these charts! You have reached the highest level of pop. Well, for this book at least. How did you get all those codes? And you're a pro at pop teasers! Congratulations on your pop IQ!

Celebrity ?uiz-o-rama